THE CHRISTMAS LETTER

BY
LOREE LOUGH

Published 2022 by Progressive Rising Phoenix Press, LLC
www.progressiverisingphoenix.com

ISBN: 978-1-958640-27-2

Printed in the U.S.A.

Edited by Mary Alford

Cover photo: "Amish Buggy in Winter stock photo" by David Arment, iStock Photo ID: 1224706144, used under license from iStock.com.

Cover design by Amanda Thrasher and William Speir

Book design by William Speir
Visit: http://www.williamspeir.com

CHAPTER 1

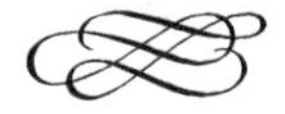

Beth ran a gloved hand across her forehead. “Someone needs to tell the calendar that it’s June, not August. Tomorrow, I’ll take the box fan out of my kitchen window and put it—”

“That would only push the hot air around. And have us sweeping sawdust and cushion stuffing from every corner.”

She frowned. Mercifully, Ben didn’t see it, because as usual, he’d responded without looking up from the workbench. They’d been sharing projects for nearly three months now, more than enough time for her to have grown accustomed to his sometimes brusque behavior.

Don’t be petty, Beth. He’s quite pleasant... most of the time. And on a more practical level, his idea to blend their talents—woodworking and upholstery— had increased her bank balance considerably.

“How are you coming with that welting?”

"Just a few more yards to go." Soon, she'd embellish the blue damask cushions with matching cording, and God willing, the Baltimore-based customer would be so pleased with the end result that she'd tell her friends, who'd bring more orders to the unique partnership between Luttwyler Antiques & Collectibles and Nip 'n' Tuck Upholstery.

Ben stepped away from the lathe and held up the cabriole leg. "Now I ask you," he said, squinting at its curve, "why would any sane person want eight chairs, all with feet shaped like Christmas trees?"

When he put it that way, it did seem a bit silly. But the lady had been so sweet that Beth felt guilty admitting it.

"Mrs. Symington told me that her entire house has a Christmas theme, year 'round. Wreaths, garlands, stars, trees, all decorated with ornaments and twinkle lights of a different color scheme for every room."

Ben's dark eyebrows drew together. "Good grief. Can you picture that?"

Actually, she could. Every Christmas since she'd purchased the cottage at the edge of town, Beth had adhered to Plain rules, draping unadorned pine swags from the porch rails, trimming candles with holly branches for the mantel and tables, and centering a Cyprus wreath in the front door's window. If these simple decorations had the power to brighten up the place, how much more festive would the house look with the addition of shimmering glass balls and sparkling lights?

"Why do folks need a reminder every year that the emphasis should be on Christ's birth," Ben was saying, "not gaudy decorations and mounds of gifts they cannot afford."

She'd heard it all before. More often than not, it preceded complaints about the community's gradual shift from Old Order to New Order ways, and reminded Beth that these traits mirrored her father's… and explained why Thomas avoided her house at Christmastime. Daily, she prayed for the strength to forgive and forget how miserable those traits had made her mother, right up until the day she'd died.

Annoyed now, Beth considered a reminder of her own: New Order ways allowed power tools, gas-powered engines, appliances, and made every Pleasant Valley business owner's work easier. *Lord, clear my mind of negative thoughts.* She decided to concentrate on Ben's finer qualities: Devotion to his parents, twin sisters, and their families, was surpassed only by his commitment to God. And she'd never known him to say no to a friend in need. As long as the Old Order versus New Order lifestyles didn't come up, he was easy to work with.

So easy, in fact, that on occasion, Beth allowed herself to daydream about what life might be like if, in addition to being partners in business, they were partners in *life*…

"Thank the good Lord the woman is not *my* wife."

…and then he'd say something like that and hurl her right back to reality.

She remembered the customer well. The lady had been friendly, and respectful of Amish ways, right down to her modest attire. Beth couldn't say the same for many visitors to Pleasant Valley, whose conduct and clothing were anything *but* Plain. If her neighbors—or disapproving *daed*—passed judgment on the *Englishers*, Beth discreetly mentioned Matthew 7:1. She wanted to say something like that now. To *Ben*. Instead, she whispered, "'Show hospitality to one another without grumbling.'"

He turned to face her. "First Peter, chapter four, verse nine."

"I meant no offense," Beth admitted.

"None taken, because you are right." One broad shoulder lifted in a brief shrug. "I should not judge her. Or her poor husband." Ben winced slightly, scrubbed a hand over his face. "I know, I know. Guilty again." He paused. "But I meant no offense."

Oh, how she loved the way his entire face got involved when he smiled! Beth decided, then and there, to find ways to encourage more of it.

"Remember that lady who wanted us to repair and reupholster that big, ugly chaise lounge?"

"How could I forget?" Ben raised his voice several octaves in a clumsy attempt at duplicating the woman's directive: "'Make it look like something Marilyn Monroe might sit upon, while reading movie scripts.'"

They shared a moment of companionable laughter, and in the ensuing silence, his gaze locked to hers. He stared, unblinking, for a full six seconds— Beth knew, because she counted as he crossed the room. Ben stopped mere inches from the sewing machine.

Leaning in close, he said, "I thought so," and plucked a bit of thread from her eyelashes.

Beth held her breath and remembered another customer who, just last week, delivered a bolt of crimson Baronet satin to be used in re-covering his wife's favorite chair. In all her years of working with fabric, Beth had never felt anything as smooth and rich. Ben's voice, she thought as he straightened, sounded like that satin felt.

Well, don't just sit here like a lovestruck schoolgirl. Say something!

"Thank you," she managed.

His left brow lifted. So did one corner of his mouth. And then he winked. Winked! Was Ben… was he *flirting* with her? No. That couldn't be. He'd always followed *Ordnung* rules to the letter and knew full well that flirtation invited disapproval.

"I hate to think what might have happened if it ended up in your beautiful—"

He stopped speaking so suddenly that Beth wondered if he'd accidentally inhaled the offending thread. Red-faced and silent, he drove a hand through dark, collar-length waves. Beth hated seeing him so uncomfortable, especially since saving her from possible eye irritation had caused it.

Ben returned to his workbench to continue hand-sanding the chair legs.

~

"In case you were wondering, I am not opposed to *Christmas.* I agree that it is a time of celebration throughout the world. What I disagree with is that, around here, the New Order attempts to celebrate it on December 25th, instead of January 6th. Old Christmas commemorates the three wise men, going to Bethlehem to find the baby Jesus." Beth didn't reply. Had she even heard him? A quick glance over his shoulder confirmed she had. She held his gaze. "According to one of my regular customers—and although I haven't verified this, it sounds accurate—the 25th coincided with the pagan celebration of the winter solstice. He said that in 1582, based on phases of the moon, the *Englishers* traded the Julian calendar for the Gregorian, and ever since, Protestants have celebrated Christmas on the 25th."

One of his regulars had told him the same things, including, "Many of those Protestant groups, including our Anabaptist ancestors, still refuse to acknowledge what they consider a pagan ritual."

"Silly, isn't it, that some Amish sects are pushing for a change, while others hold fast to the 6th? Seems we should all be on the same page." She hid a smile behind one hand. "Calendar page, that is."

"Another thing we Amish should drop is all the commercialization; stick to paying homage in the Plain way. Stop all the decorating and gift-giving, too, and simply honor His birth."

Her smile gone now, Beth pretended intense concentration on the welting. No doubt she thought the steady hum of her sewing machine drowned out her words. "I'm afraid we'll never agree on that," she muttered, hunched over the old Singer.

He'd rescued the machine a year or so ago, tucked among overflowing trash cans, a threadbare mattress, and a bent-up lawn chair whose webbing had seen better days. Several hours of sanding and a coat of varnish restored the pine cabinet to its original sheen, but it had taken a full day to repair the machine itself.

"You have such a big, lovely family," she was saying now. "Surely you get together for a holiday meal."

"I am all in favor of such gatherings. It's worry over what gifts to buy them that annoys me. Wasted time and money, if you ask me."

"So you exchange gifts?"

"Yes, which obliges me to choose something for each of them, a task I dread every year."

"The presents don't have to cost money," Beth said. "With your carpentry skills, you could make them from scrap wood."

He faced Beth, matched her disapproving expression with one of his own.

"Those are the *only* gifts I give. But making them not only takes time from work that puts money in the bank, it requires me to purchase paper and ribbon to wrap them up."

"Rest easy, Ben. This year, bring them to my house. I'll wrap them the way I wrap mine, using fabric scraps. That way, you'll have nothing to complain about."

Now she looked downright smug, and he didn't like it one bit.

"If I need help, I will let you know." *But do not hold your breath!*

If she'd heard the sarcasm in his voice, Beth showed no sign of it.

"My best friend Martha has a subscription to the *Holmes County Shopper*. Once she's read it, she shares it with me. I read an article about members of the Old Order Amish church in Ohio. The writer quoted a man who felt that the younger generation is all about education and reading and making improvements that add to the family coffers. In his opinion, their elders would keep doing things the Old Order way, simply because that's the way they'd always done things. He feared the youngsters would soon celebrate Christmas on the 25th, causing bad feelings among their elders, who'd stick with the 6th?" One delicate brow lifted as she added, "I suppose you agree with them."

Until today, Beth had been upbeat and agreeable. This was a side of her he hadn't seen before, and Ben wasn't at all sure he liked it. He definitely had no idea how to respond to her last comment.

"Fascinating, isn't it," she said, "that a tradition that began so very long ago could still be so important these days!"

He went back to sanding the chair leg. *Fascinating that all these centuries later, it still has the power to cause controversy among friends.*

Loree Lough

Friends…

Despite the disagreement, Ben wanted to be more than just her friend. So much more! But could they find a way to come to terms with vastly different beliefs about, of all things, *Christmas?*

CHAPTER 2

Ben had promised to deliver the tree-footed table and chairs to Baltimore today, and since Beth had seemed so fond of the customer, he stopped at her house to see if she'd like to make the trip with him. He hadn't seen her in days. Had she been avoiding him because of the Christmas discussion? He hoped not, because he missed her.

He found her bent over her checkbook, looking frazzled, muttering. It was a relief when she looked up and smiled at the sight of him. His relief doubled when his invitation compelled her to say, "What a great excuse to get my mind off… money." Standing, she tossed the pen onto the desk.

"Better take a jacket," he suggested. "There's a nip in the air today."

She grasped a thick sweater from the hook beside the door. "Well,

I suppose unpredictable weather is the price we pay for our beautiful Allegheny Mountain views, isn't it?" Halfway out the door, she darted back inside, grabbed two water bottles from the fridge, handed one to Ben, and picked up a bag of chips. Barbecue. His favorite. Yet another 'something' they had in common.

From the moment she slid onto the front seat until they arrived at the customer's house, Beth talked. And talked. About the weather, her latest customer, the troubles she'd been having trying to order special fabric for the job. Beth told him that when she'd gone into town for groceries, she'd run into one of his twin sisters, and they chatted for such a long time that Rebecca's ice cream nearly melted. In between announcements, she asked about him: As a boy, did he have a dog? "No," he replied, "my mother was allergic to animal fur." Had he been a good student? "English wasn't my forte," he said, "but I held my own in Math." Beth nodded at each reply, as if making mental Ben Notes. He'd so enjoyed the trip and friendly conversation that when they reached their destination, Ben had to fight disappointment.

"Oh my," Beth said as he backed into the driveway. "Looks like Mrs. Symington's love of Christmas isn't limited to the inside of her house. It's spilled into the lawn and gardens!"

And it was true. No matter where his gaze landed, Ben saw evidence of the woman's affection for the holiday: Santas, elves, reindeer, candy canes, and stars decorated the porch and shrubs.

The woman called her teenage son to help Ben move the furniture from his truck to the red-painted dining room, where the tree-shaped feet of the table and chairs nearly disappeared into thick green carpeting.

"I love it!" Mrs. Symington gushed. "It's even more beautiful than I expected!"

"Just what we need around here," her son teased, "*more* Christmas junk."

Undaunted, his mother wrote a check, adding a hundred dollars to the agreed-upon amount, and sent them on their way with a brown bag filled to the brim with iced Christmas cookies. In July!

Minutes later, as Ben steered onto I-695, Beth said, "She's one customer I'll never forget. I won't forget this traffic, either."

"It is rush hour," he said. "Happens every day at this time and in the morning, too."

"Oh, these poor people. How do they stand it?" She plucked a Santa-shaped cookie from the bag, handed it to Ben. "Aren't we blessed that our only traffic—if you want to call it that—is when Homer's old tractor putts along Pleasant Valley Road?"

Yes, he felt blessed, all right, and not just because the community's roads were devoid of congestion.

"Your sister offered to help me with the costumes for the children's Christmas pageant."

"She did? When?"

"When I ran into her at Food Lion, of course."

"Ah-ha. Of course." Oh, she was a marvel. Even if he had the power to change her, Ben wouldn't.

He bit off the pom-pom on Santa's hat. "What will she sew?" he said around it.

"Hems, mostly. I don't have much patience for hand-stitching."

"What!" Ben laughed. "Your upholstery business is nothing *but* hand stitching!"

"Well, yes, sort of, but… but that's different. Big fat needles with great big eyes, thick thread, sturdy material… easy peasy."

"Easy peasy," he echoed. "Where did you pick up *that* term?"

"You know, I have no idea." She crunched into a cookie. "Mind if I ask you a question?"

"You can ask. I cannot promise a satisfactory answer."

"I've noticed that you never use contractions. Not 'I've,' but 'I have.' Instead of 'don't,' you say 'do not.' Never can't. With you, it's 'cannot.' Is it one way to cling to Old Order ways?"

Ben gave it a moment's thought. "I suppose that explains it as well as anything." *Although I am not fond of the word* cling.

Beth took another bite of her star-shaped cookie, used it as a pointer.

"Using contractions saves time, you know, especially when writing."

"But, Beth, what would I do with all the time I save using apostrophes?"

She seemed too busy collecting crumbs from her apron to hear him. Beth dropped them into an upturned palm and rolled down the window. "The birds will love this," she said, and flung them into the wind… which blew them right back into her lap.

Laughing quietly, Ben said, “I will say this for you, Beth Lantz, there is never a moment of boredom when you are around.”

“Hmm…” She unscrewed the cap of her water bottle. “Did I tell you I volunteered to sew costumes for the schoolchildren’s annual Christmas pageant?”

“Yes, on the way to Baltimore.”

“Oh yes. I did, didn’t I?” She took a sip. Another sip, and then, “And that I had to order faux fur for some of them?”

“For the sheep, cows, and donkeys, right?”

She nodded.

“Did I tell you I’m making booths for the Harvest Festival?”

“You are? Oh, Ben, how nice of you, especially since it’s only a few weeks off.” She hid a yawn behind one dainty hand, rested her head against the window, and promptly fell asleep.

Chuckling under his breath, Ben said, “I take it back. There are a *few* boring moments with you.”

CHAPTER 3

Three days after the trip to Baltimore, Ben conducted a quick inventory of his materials. His supply of nails had diminished, and he noticed a chip in the tip of his favorite chisel. Much as he disliked driving into Oakland, he made a trip to the hardware store.

After purchasing a new chisel and boxes of common, finishing, and framing nails, he stopped at the Sip 'n' Dine. Ben had just stepped up to the order counter when a booming voice said, "Benjamin!"

He turned, looked into the bearded face of Beth's father. "Good to see you, Thomas."

"Good to see you, too. Get your coffee and join Mark and me."

Ben started to explain he'd planned to take his to go, but Thomas said, "We are sitting right there, near the windows."

Mark lifted a hand in a half-hearted wave, his sheepish expression offering an apology of sorts. Ben nodded, his way of saying "None needed."

He'd barely settled into the chair facing them when Thomas said, "You have been spending much time with my daughter, yes?"

"Working on several shared projects, yes."

"She told me about her involvement in the school's annual pageant. Are you involved with it as well?"

Ben shook his head. "I have been asked to stabilize the risers and repair hinges on the manger. But what I know about sewing would not fit in a thimble, so Beth and I will work separately."

Mark grinned. His father did not.

"I have tried and tried," Thomas said, "but the girl is as stubborn as Floyd's mule. Her Christmas obsession grows with each passing year." He exhaled a heavy sigh. "Takes after her mother that way, I am afraid."

Mark leaned both elbows on the red-marbled Formica table top. "Beth honors your feelings about Christmas, *Daed*, and the decorations she displays at her house are well within Plain rules. She does so much for us, and even the bishop approves of what Beth is doing for the school. Why can't we just let her enjoy the holiday?"

Thomas turned slightly and glared at his son. "When I want your opinion, Son, I will ask for it."

Mark had made a valid point, but Ben wanted no part of this dispute.

"How are things at the farm, Thomas?"

Hands up in mock surrender, Thomas said, "All right, all right. I will speak no more about Beth."

"Good," Mark said quietly. "Because it isn't right, bad-mouthing her when she isn't here to defend herself."

Either Thomas hadn't heard his son, or he'd chosen to overlook the borderline irreverent remark.

"It has been a good year," Thomas told Ben. "This spring's shearing brought many pounds of wool, and the sheep are already well on their way to growing thick new coats. God willing, next year will be better still."

"Good, good," Ben said. Meeting Mark's eyes, he added, "And did the *Englishers* keep you busy this year?"

A few days a week, Beth's brother made extra money by taking tourists on guided fishing expeditions. Many times, Ben had been tempted to book an excursion himself.

"Oh, yes. I spent more time in Cumberland this summer than here in Pleasant Valley."

"I hope you left some trout in Wills Creek for the rest of us."

"Say the word, and I'll show you where to find plenty." The younger man snickered. "For a price."

Ben laughed, but Thomas didn't so much as crack a smile. Evidently, Ben thought, Mark and Beth had inherited their sense of humor from their mother.

"Well, much as I have enjoyed catching up," he said, standing, "I have jobs waiting at the warehouse."

"Jobs that involve my daughter?"

"No upholstery on this one." *Unfortunately,* Ben thought. And before either of the men could respond, he wished them well and hustled to the door.

CHAPTER 4

Ben was hard at work, putting the finishing touches on a light-ed curio cabinet, when the bell alerted him that someone had entered the shop. Dusting his hands on a vinegar-soaked rag, he entered the office area of his warehouse. There stood Beth, hands clasped primly at her waist. "Well, hi, stranger."

"Hi, yourself." She adjusted her *kapp*. "So windy out there. I hope it doesn't mean there's a storm on the way."

"If those dark clouds over Backbone Mountain are any gauge, we might see thunder and lightning this afternoon." He slid both hands into the wide pocket of his work apron. "Are you here with good news? Another project to work on together?"

"No."

A tiny half-smile produced a dainty dimple in her right cheek. Why hadn't he noticed it before now? But why had she come to see him?

And why did she look so… anxious? Had her father delivered another high-minded lesson about Christmas and all things related?

"Is everything all right?"

"Yes, but—but I… I'd like to run something by you."

"I am on a deadline. Mind if we talk while I work?"

"Not at all." she followed him into the workshop. When Beth saw the curio cabinet, she ran fingertips along the intricately carved trim. "Oh, Ben. All of your work is beautiful, but you've outdone yourself this time."

Pointing, he indicated the odd-shaped box in the far corner. "Curved glass," he explained. "Special order, and costly." He drew her attention to the groove that would hold it in place. "It will be a challenge, making sure it fits perfectly, that it will stay in place when the door opens and closes."

She nodded, and when she did, a glossy curl escaped from beneath her *kapp*.

"Yes, I can see how important that'll be." Beth met his eyes. "If I thought I could be of any help…" She punctuated the offer with a tiny shrug.

"No worries. It will come together."

"Of course it will. Your woodworking talents are unrivaled."

"Better stop," he said, "or I will have to carve keyhole shapes in all the doorways, to make sure I will not clunk my swollen head on the jambs."

Beth laughed, but only a little. Clearly, something was troubling her. Grasping his smallest chisel, Ben went back to carving the channel that would hold the curved class in place. "So what can I do for you today?"

"I just came from the schoolhouse. I was measuring the children. You know, for their costumes? The ones I'll sew for the Christmas pageant? Well, I… I was measuring one girl, and she… she wanted to know…" Beth groaned, hid behind her hands. "This is so awkward. I don't quite know how to put it."

He stopped working and faced her. "Did her question involve me?"

"Yes. Sort of. And… it's about me, too."

Ben put the chisel down. "You will feel better if you just get it off your chest." *And so will I!*

"She… she asked if we were married."

"*Married!* Whatever gave her that idea?"

"She said because we work together, alone, we must be husband and wife." A schoolgirl wouldn't have come up with a notion like that all on her own. She'd overheard an adult conversation, one that had concentrated on him and Beth. He could almost hear the busybodies reciting *Ordnung* courtship rules, passed down through the ages, stating that unmarried men and women should never spend time together without a chaperone.

"Beth, we *work* together. Earn *money* together. You know as well as I that cash payments always overrule other Amish rules."

Based on her serious expression, Beth didn't get the joke. To help her see she was worrying over nothing, Ben lowered his voice, looked left and right. "We are alone right now," he whispered. "Did you take precautions, make sure no one saw you come in?"

Big eyes grew bigger still as she turned the question over in her mind. Upon realizing he'd been teasing, Beth feigned a stern frown. "This is hardly a laughing matter, Ben."

"I know, I know." He rested a hand on her shoulder and gave it an affectionate squeeze. "But I think people have better things to do than keep tabs on the time we spend"—he wiggled his eyebrows—"together. Alone." Now her eyes sparkled with relief. And a bit of mischief.

Ben wrapped the wayward curl around his forefinger, took a half-step closer. "I can never decide whether your eyes are brown or green."

"They're hazel, and change, depending on the weather and the color of my clothes."

It felt good, seeing that he'd calmed her fears, but for a reason he couldn't explain, her worries had transferred to him. She was one of the most capable, independent women he knew, yet Ben wanted to protect her, from town gossips, from hardship, from every negative thing life threw her way.

"Have any customers asked you to fix things that require upholstery?"

The question reminded him of how she'd looked the other day, when he walked into her shop and saw her frowning at her checkbook.

"No, but this is only a temporary dry spell, for both of us."

She glanced at the curio cabinet. At the buffet behind it. And the bed frame beside that. "Unless these are your own pieces, you're not suffering a dry spell!"

"I have not been paid for any of these."

"Yet."

If she was *your wife, she would have no need to worry about money.*

The thought rocked him. Ben took a quick step back. Beth must have read it to mean that she'd kept him from his work long enough.

"Thank you for listening," she said, and started walking toward the door.

"You can talk to me any time. About anything."

Her pace slowed a bit as he added, "I mean it."

"You're a good friend, Ben Luttwyler. I'm blessed to know you." With that, Beth left.

She'd been gone less than a minute, yet he missed her already.

He treasured their friendship, but Ben wished yet again that they could be more than that.

A whole lot more.

CHAPTER 5

The next afternoon, Beth stood at her kitchen counter, rolling dough for the pie she'd bring to dinner at her father's house this Sunday. She'd already prepared the main course, and the beef stew now simmered on the stove. Its hearty aroma floated through the cottage as she wondered whether to top it off with dumplings or biscuits.

A soft knock drew her attention from the raw crust, and she opened the back door.

"Martha, what a nice surprise," she said, waving her friend inside. "What brings you out and about on this blustery day?"

"Blustery is right. I'd think that storm would have taken the wind when it ended." She gave her umbrella a good shake and closed it. "I have good news and couldn't wait another minute to share it."

"Sit and tell me all about it while I get us some coffee."

Martha pressed a palm to her stomach. "No thanks. I still love the stuff, but it doesn't like me these days."

These days? Beth wiped floury hands on a red-checked tea towel. Martha and Paul had been married slightly more than five years, and their only disappointment seemed to be the inability to have a child.

"Are you… are you *pregnant*?"

Blushing, Martha said, "Can you believe it? I guess the good Lord grew tired of hearing us say, 'Please, send us a baby!'"

Beth drew her into a sisterly hug. "I'm so happy for you. And for Paul. He must be beside himself with joy." She pulled out a chair. "Sit. I'll make tea, instead. Can you tolerate tea? You're all right, aren't you?"

"I'm fine, just fine, and yes, I can still drink tea."

Beth turned up the fire under the kettle, then slid two mugs from the cupboard. "How long have you known?"

"Only a few weeks. I didn't want to tell anyone until I was sure. Emily knows, since she's my doctor, and Paul, of course. But I haven't even told my parents yet."

"I'm honored to be in on the secret." Beth dropped a teabag into each mug, then poured milk into a tiny white pitcher. "I'm thrilled for you," she said again, "just thrilled."

Martha looked around. "Don't stop working on my account. Your crust will dry out. And I'm perfectly capable of pouring water into cups."

"A sprinkle of water will revive the dough. Maybe you can help me decide between biscuits and dumplings."

"Oh, biscuits. I've never tasted any as good as yours."

"It's my mother's recipe. She deserves the credit." Beth grasped Martha's hand, squeezed it. "Mother. In a few short months, *you'll* be a mother! When is the baby due?"

"Emily says mid-March. Late March, maybe. So let's pray the mountains won't decide to bury us in snow, like they did last year!"

"They wouldn't dare."

The kettle whistled, and Beth turned off the burner, and as she placed both mugs on the table, Martha asked, "Are you still working with Mr. Handsome?"

The word described him as accurately as any, Beth thought. "Not lately. Seems neither of us have had any requests for furniture repairs that require upholstery."

"What a shame. Bet you're disappointed."

"Why?"

Martha laughed, reached across the table and patted Beth's hand. "Oh come on now. I've known you too long for you to try and fool me. I've seen the way you look at him, and the way he looks at you. You're crazy about one another."

"The way we..." Beth swallowed. Hard. "You saw us? Together?"

"Only by accident. I saw the pair of you in church. Why, you could hang clothes out to dry on the invisible line between your eyes and his."

"What!"

"He stares at you all through the service." Martha clucked her tongue.

"Don't tell me you never noticed!"

To be honest, Beth had caught him looking her way from time to time. But she'd hardly call that *staring*.

"I walked past his shop one day, and you two were busy trying to attach some sort of cushion—blue, as I recall—to a big, overstuffed chair. Why, even his *voice* changes when he talks to you."

"His..." Beth swallowed again. "It changes? How?"

"It's softer, gentler, and he can't seem to take his eyes off you. Not even when he's supposed to be sanding table legs."

How long did you stand and watch, oh friend of mine? Beth wondered. Quite a while, if she'd seen and heard all that!

"No need to look embarrassed, dear sweet Beth. You're perfect for each other. *Perfect,* I tell you. Why, I'll bet in a year or two, you'll be telling *me* that a baby's on the way."

Married. To Ben. With a baby on the way. It was a beautiful picture, for sure.

Martha sipped her tea, wrinkled her nose. "Good grief. I left the teabag in too long. And forgot to add sugar." She got to her feet. "Just as well. I need to get home and start supper. And you need to get back to that pie dough before it turns to leather." She gave Beth a sideways hug. "See you soon, I hope."

And with that, Martha left. Beth had just slid the pies into the oven when a shiny black SUV rolled into her driveway. She stood at the window, watching as a young man made his way up the walk.

"I hate to bother you, but would you mind taking a look at this couch thing in the back of my truck, see if it's worth saving?"

Beth set the oven timer, dropped it into her apron pocket, and followed him outside. He lifted the vehicle's hatch to reveal a nearly threadbare settee.

"It belonged to my fiancée's grandmother. She's gone now. Couple months back, I bought her house as a surprise wedding present. I was close to finishing the renovations when I found this in the basement, hidden behind a wall of boxes behind the furnace. Saw a picture of my fiancée sitting on her grandmother's lap on the old thing. She looked so happy. I thought it would make a nice addition to the stuff I've been buying. You know, something familiar and meaningful."

"What a loving, thoughtful gift." Oh, how she wished someone loved her enough to go to all that trouble!

"So do you think it can be fixed? Or should I drive straight to the dump?"

"If I remove everything, right down to the frame…"

"What if, when you get down to the bare wood, it's not worth the bother?"

"Just so happens I know someone who's a very talented woodworker."

Friend. If Martha had been right, might she and Ben become more than—

"Should I carry it inside, then?"

"Yes, please do. There's a dolly in my shop. Let me get it, to make moving it a little easier."

Fifteen minutes later, Beth gave the settee a closer look. Yes, she believed she could bring it back to as-new condition. She showed him a book of upholstery samples, and he chose a muted blue, yellow, and white plaid. "Sally's favorite color is blue," he said, "and mine is yellow. So this oughta work." He met Beth's eyes. "Do you think the material will stand up to the abuse kids might give it?"

"Unless they're wearing football cleats, yes."

He laughed, then sniffed the air. "Mmm. Something smells good."

"I have pies in the oven. And stew on the stove."

He smacked his lips. "I sure hope Sally'll learn to cook like that." He slid a weathered brown billfold from the back pocket of his jeans. "How much?" Beth did some quick mental calculations and stated a price.

"How much do you need as a deposit?"

She'd seen one thin bill in the wallet. Unless he had a wad of cash in another pocket, the young fellow might be down to his last ten dollars.

"You look trustworthy." She handed him an order tablet. "Write down your name and phone number, and I'll call when I'm finished. You can pay me when you pick it up."

"Wow. Really?" He hesitated. "But, wait… I thought you people didn't believe in phones."

You people. Beth almost laughed. "A lot of us here in Pleasant Valley have phones. Mostly for business. Some of us have cell phones, too."

Once he'd gone, Beth gave the settee another once-over, and hoped that after she stripped off the old brocade and stuffing, she'd have something, anything that would give her a bona fide reason to ask for Ben's help.

Because she just *had* to find out whether or not Martha had been seeing things!

CHAPTER 6

Ben got onto his hands and knees to inspect the settee's frame. He gave it a good shake and said, "It seems sturdy enough, but you're right. It can use new screws at the joints. I will get right on it. Might take a day or two for the glue to dry, though." He got to his feet. "Did you give the guy a delivery date?"

"I said I'd call when it's done, but I got the impression he'd like it sooner rather than later." She pointed at the thick roll of batting and the bolt of plaid fabric the young man had picked, and she explained his reasons for the choice. "I'm undecided about trimming the arms and cushion with welting. What do you think?"

Ben dusted both palms on the seat of his jeans. "Knowing you, the price you quoted was far less than what your time is worth. Maybe that will help you decide?"

Arms folded across her chest, Beth shrugged. "I have blue fabric that will match exactly, and more than enough cording." Nodding, she added, "Yeah, I think I'll add welting. It'll look so much better. He mentioned children in the future, so the trim will make the edges sturdier, too."

"Want me to bring it to my shop to work on it? Get it out of your way?"

"No need for that. The only thing I'm working on right now is the pageant. And as you know, my sewing machine is in the other room, so you won't be in the way."

Thank You, Lord, Ben prayed, because now he'd have the perfect excuse to spend a few hours with her each day.

"How about a slice of pie?"

"Have you ever known me to say no to that question?"

It was a short walk to the rooms at the back of the house that she'd turned into her shop and storeroom. In the kitchen, she said, "Did your customer pick up that curio cabinet yet?"

"No, she will have to wait until early next week. I added adhesive in the groove that holds the glass in place. Without it, one good slam and it could pop out."

"And you say *I'm* guilty of giving customers extra service for free."

He sat at the table and glanced around the homey kitchen. "How long have you lived here?"

"Nearly three years."

"I am impressed."

"Ah, remembering what it looked like four years ago, hmm?" She plated the pie and delivered it with a napkin and fork. "Coffee?"

"Milk, if you have some." He cut off the point of the slice. "And yes, I remember how it used to look. Every time I drove past it, I shook my head, wondering how anyone could walk away from what had been their home, without a thought or a care about what might become of it."

Beth brought his milk and sat across from him. "I felt the same way, until I found out that after Jonah Wagler lost his family in a buggy accident, he went to live with relatives in Ohio. Too many memories here, I suppose. He'd put the bishop in charge of the sale, and when I heard the asking price, I jumped at the chance to buy it."

"Even knowing how much work it would take to make it livable?"

"Even knowing."

They sat in companionable silence for a minute or two.

"Did it cost much, hiring laborers to do the work?"

"Laborers." She laughed. "My brother promised to help if I'd do his laundry and make fudge once a week. How could I pass that up?"

"You mean the two of you did the work?"

"It didn't happen overnight, but yes, using materials people threw out and 'seconds' from the lumber yard."

She described the process, from removing damaged plaster and replacing it with drywall, to hanging new windows and doors. Her least favorite job? Replacing the roof. Her favorite? The completion of her wrap-around porch.

"If I had a quarter for every blister, splinter, and callus I earned during the repairs, I could have paid poor Mark for all his help."

"Something tells me he feels good, knowing he helped put you into a well-built home of your own."

"Yes, I believe you're right. Would you like a tour of the place?"

He almost asked, "What if someone saw me arrive and reports us for violating the 'no chaperone' rule?", but thought better of it.

"I would like to see the rest of it."

Beth showed him the parlor, decorated in Plain colors, but thanks to careful furniture placement, starched white curtains, and wildflower arrangements on the tables, it felt warm and welcoming. The same was true upstairs, where the bathroom and three bedrooms all but shouted, "Come in and make yourself at home." And the basement's gray-painted floor, white cinderblock walls, and overhead beams looked bright and cheerful.

Back in the kitchen, he drained the last of the milk from the glass and finished the pie. "That really hit the spot, but I should—"

"You're… you aren't leaving already, are you?"

If only he could think of a valid reason to stay.

Beth said, "I'd hoped we could talk about the Harvest Festival."

"Oh?"

"I was thinking we might share a booth. You know, fix up a few pieces of furniture, showcase our respective talents, and maybe drum up a little business in the process."

He had to admit that it was a pretty good idea. "I volunteered to build some booths. Why not make one for us while I am at it?"

"Yes, why not?"

"We do work well together. A real cooperative team."

Beth inhaled a sharp breath, and hands clasped under her chin, said, "That gives me an idea for our sign. I'll paint 'L&L Cooperative' at the top, and beneath it, in smaller letters, 'Luttwyler & Lantz, Making the Old New Again.' It must be divine providence that we have the same initials, don't you think?" He loved the way her mind worked. He loved her energy, her positive nature. He'd never heard mention of her middle name, but he guessed it might be *Enthusiastic*.

"I am sure the sign will look wonderful. Everything you touch turns out wonderfully."

"Ben, stop, or I'll have to spend an hour on my knees, begging God's forgiveness for my sin of pride."

He carried his plate and glass to the sink. "What I said is true. Your talents are gifts from God, after all. Being thankful for those blessings… how can that be sinful?"

"Thanks for your encouragement." Beth paused, aimed a playful grin his way. "Now, if only you were as open-minded about Christmas…"

A few months ago, a remark like that might have annoyed him. Right now, it made him want to take her in his arms, press his lips to hers, and recite all the things he loved about her. It took every ounce of willpower to walk to the door.

"Thanks again for the snack." One hand on the doorknob, he added, "If it is all right with you, I will be back first thing in the morning. The sooner I get that settee frame secured, the sooner your young bridegroom-to-be can deliver his surprise wedding gift."

"All right with me? Why, that sounds wonderful. I'll make breakfast. Pancakes or waffles?"

"No need to feed—"

"I will make breakfast," she repeated, emphasizing each word.

"All right then. Pancakes it is."

The last thing he heard before revving the pickup's engine was her sweet voice saying, "I'm up by six…"

Ben shifted into drive and aimed the truck toward home.

The tiny apartment he'd walled-off at the rear of his warehouse held a bed, dresser, small table and chairs, sink, mini fridge and stove, even a three-piece bathroom. But after spending time at Beth's house, where the scent of Ivory soap filled the air and quilts covered the beds, Ben found it difficult to call the place home.

Admit it, Luttwyler. You want a home with Beth.

The thought had come as naturally as breathing. Coupled with the many times he'd dreamed of walking with her, talking to her, working beside her…

You've fallen in love with her, you fool!

The admission inspired a smirk.

Should he admit to *Beth* that he'd unconsciously used a contraction?

Perhaps it was a sign that she was part of God's will for his life… and he for hers…

CHAPTER 7

Ben saw Beth, standing outside the church, talking with Martha and Paul. He hadn't seen her since the day of the Harvest Festival, when they'd worked side by side, greeting locals and tourists who'd traveled for miles to attend the annual event. How lovely she looked in her dark wool coat, even with her shoulders hunched against the cold wind. He willed her to look his way, so he could wave good morning.

She did more than that. The moment she spotted him, Beth descended the steps and stopped a few feet away.

"Where have you been keeping yourself?" he asked.

One hand on her head to keep her *kapp* from blowing away, she said, "Home, finishing up the pageant costumes."

"Finishing? It is not even Thanksgiving yet!"

"The children were so excited to see one another dressed up as angels and the animals of the Nativity that I wanted to get them done quickly. Besides, it wasn't as though I've been overloaded with upholstery jobs."

A gust nearly took his hat, but he caught it just in time. "My business has been sluggish, too."

"Maybe if I'd painted the second line of our sign in bigger letters—who we are and what we do—potential customers might have remembered us."

"And if I had printed up business cards to hand out, the way so many of our neighbors did, we could have handed them out when people stopped to look at our projects."

"Well, at least we sold everything, right?"

"Yes, despite the foul weather."

Ben remembered how the on-again, off-again rain had discouraged the usual crowds. The few who'd braved the damp, biting breezes hadn't stood long at any of the booths. Bundled up to keep warm and dry, not even funnel cakes and corn dogs, or testing handmade windmill toys captured their interest. Many of their neighbors had packed up early, but he and Beth stayed until sundown. Not even the bitter cold that stiffened his fingers and blew stinging rain against his cheeks had made him want to leave. And to her credit, Beth hadn't complained either.

Her father and brother walked past just then, interrupting the pleasant memory.

"The two of you must be daft. It cannot be more than twenty degrees out here," Thomas said over one shoulder. "Why are you out here?" He hurried toward the steps and into the church.

Because inside, Ben thought, he'd have to share Beth with the rest of the community. And she'd have to sit all the way on the other side of the building with the women and children.

Mark winked at her. "*Daed* is right," he said, rubbing his palms together. "I'm going in, and unless your brains are too frozen to think straight, you two will follow."

Side by side, they entered the church. "Will you have your father and brother over after the service?"

When she tilted her face up to meet his eyes, he noticed that the overhead lights had caused her long lashes to paint spiky shadows on her wind-rosy cheeks. And right there, in the house of God, he fought the urge to kiss every freckle that dotted her nose.

"Martha is signaling me to sit with her." She leaned in close and whispered, "She and Paul are expecting a baby, but keep it to yourself. I don't think it's public knowledge yet."

He was careful not to look in her friend's direction. "I am happy for them," Ben said as she walked away. *And envious…*

During the past few months, he'd spent countless hours on his knees, asking God's forgiveness for prideful thoughts—mostly inspired by Beth's compliments—and for wishful thinking. Once settled in his usual place with his father, brothers-in-law, and young nephews, Ben bowed his head and prayed that those wishes were aligned with His will.

Eyes open now, he searched the women's benches and did his best not to smile once he found her. Sitting as tall as her 5′ 2″ frame would allow, she listened to something Martha had whispered into her ear. Beth hid a giggle behind one hand. It hid her whispered reply, too. Had her friend ever noticed the calluses on the palm-side of that hand? Not likely. But Ben had noticed. And every time, as he'd watched her squint to thread a big-eyed needle, or struggle to pull two sections of heavy upholstery material together, he'd thought about how much easier her life could be… as his wife. *And how much better* your *life would be, as her husband.*

The deacon took his place up front, opened the Bible, and read a passage from the book of John: "By this shall ye know that ye are my disciples, if ye have love one for another."

At that precise moment, Beth looked up, and realizing he'd been staring at her, she blinked. Smiled. Pressed both palms to her cheeks. Seeing it, Martha followed her gaze and winked at him. Sitting up straighter, Ben concentrated on the deacon. He barely heard a word, but at least he wouldn't get caught again, gawking at Beth.

Half an hour later, he worked out the kinks in his neck, kinks caused by his stubborn determination to keep his eyes off her. But when the final hymn began, he risked another glimpse, and saw that, like everything else, she put her heart and soul into singing. He'd always loved the musical lilt of her voice. How much more lovely might it be in song?

Peripheral vision told him that Martha had sent another wink in his direction. Ben didn't care. *Lord,* he prayed, *if Beth isn't in Your will for me, show me a sign.*

Beth chose that moment to look his way again. Almost immediately, her cheeks turned pink again, and this time, the weather hadn't caused it. The heat of a blush crept up his neck, too, and didn't stop until his whole face felt hot. Had others, like Martha, noticed? So be it. Because if that wasn't love beaming from Beth's eyes, Ben didn't know how to describe it.

It was time to tell her that while he valued their closeness, he wanted—no, he *needed*—more than what friendship offered.

CHAPTER 8

Beth had grown tired of her winter-white kitchen walls, and thanks to careful budgeting, she could finally afford to paint them. She stood at the samples aisle, trying to decide between pale blue and butter yellow when Ben's mother stepped up beside her.

"Planning to redecorate?" she asked.

"Hannah, hello! How are you?"

"Fine, and you?"

Thanks to your son, I'm more satisfied with life than I have been in a long while. "So what are you painting?"

"Just the kitchen for now."

"I'm surprised you have time, with all that sewing you're doing. Ben told me that in addition to your usual workload, you volunteered to make costumes for the children's Christmas pageant."

If only she still had a workload, Beth thought. "Except for minor tweaks, I'm finished."

"Then he wasn't exaggerating when he called you a marvel."

He'd said that? About *her*? Beth hid her delight by plucking two paint strips from the rack. "What do you think? Yellow or blue?"

"Oh, yellow, definitely. When the sun is shining, your whole kitchen will glow!"

Beth pictured that, and liking what she saw, put the blue strip back where she'd found it.

"So what brings you to the hardware store today?"

"I finally picked all the cabbages and beets, but I used all my canning jars putting up the summer vegetables."

"I've always wanted to start a garden. There's a perfect spot behind the cottage."

"Oh, by all means, do. A garden provides so much more than food for the table." She lowered her voice. "It's a good excuse to get outside, away from the demands of family. People leave you alone, because they want no part in preparing the soil, planting, and weeding. Plus, it's the best excuse to escape mundane chores. If I put my nose to the proverbial grindstone, I'll have the job done before Thanksgiving."

"Thanksgiving." Beth sighed. "Can you believe it's only a week away?"

"This year has flown by, hasn't it?"

"I'll say!"

"What are your plans for the holiday?"

"Dinner at my father's, as usual."

"Why don't the three of you join us instead? There's plenty of room. Amos will love talking with Thomas, and our sons-in-law can catch up with Mark."

But what about Ben? Beth wondered. How would he feel about spending a major holiday with… with a coworker?

The woman must have suspected why Beth had hesitated. "Just the other day," she said, "Ben told me how much he enjoys a big crowd gathered 'round the table. 'The more, the merrier,' he said."

Distracted by a misbehaving child in the aisle, Beth could have sworn Hannah had said 'marry her.' Realizing the silly mistake, she nearly laughed out loud.

"Well, I'd better get this sample to the counter. The sooner they mix up my yellow, the sooner I can start painting. I hope you'll stop by some sunny day to see how it looks."

"I'd love that!"

The women went their separate ways, and while waiting in the checkout line, Beth remembered something Hannah had said. Shy, quiet Ben, *liked* crowds? She could hardly wait to see proof of that!

Her father and brother would likely leap at an opportunity to celebrate with friends. And when they said yes, she'd have an excuse to visit Ben, and ask him to tell Hannah that her family would join them and that she'd bring a dessert and a side.

She already knew what to bake, because Ben had told her that apple pie was his favorite.

Now to drop a few subtle hints to find out which side dishes he preferred…

CHAPTER 9

On Thanksgiving morning, Thomas knocked at her back door. She poured him a mug of coffee and slid a plate of freshly baked peanut butter cookies—his favorite—beside it.

"Thank you, *dochder.* I am afraid I will have to eat and run. One of my ewes is about to deliver, and from the look of things, the lamb is breech."

"Oh, no. Does that mean you'll have to cancel dinner with the Luttwylers?"

Her father nodded. "Yes, and I will need Mark's help, so…"

"I understand, and so will they. Just so happens there's a roasting hen in my freezer. I'll pretend it's a mini turkey. Once it's baked, I'll bring it to your house. That way, you and Mark can take turns looking in on the mother-to-be without missing out on dinner."

"Will you make stuffing?"

"Wouldn't be Thanksgiving without it!"

"Using your *mudder*'s recipe?"

"Is there any other?"

Thomas returned her smile. "You are a good woman, Beth." A silent moment passed as he sipped his coffee. Then he said, "I am disappointed that we will not eat with the Luttwylers. I had planned to find a moment to take Benjamin aside and ask what his intentions are."

"Intentions? What do you mean?"

"My eyesight is not what it once was, Beth, but I can see well enough to know he is smitten with you." He held up a hand to forestall her denial.

"Well, if that was your plan, I'm relieved we can't join them today."

A grating chuckle preceded a merry wink. "It is my duty to look out for my only *dochder*'s best interests." Squinting one eye, he added, "What do you suppose your *mudder* would say about this… your association with the Luttwyler boy?"

Beth knew exactly what Emma would say: *She'd be all for it, if it helped make her a* grossmammi.

"Women are not the only ones who look forward to *kinner,* you know."

"If God wants to make a grandfather of you, He has to orchestrate a marriage first."

Thomas helped himself to half a dozen cookies and wrapped them in a paper napkin. "Then I hope He acts quickly. You are not getting any younger, you know."

How could she forget, with his frequent reminders?

Beth took the cookies from him and dropped them, and a dozen more, into a large zipper bag. "Save a few for Mark, all right?"

He returned her smile. "If it is in God's will for the boy to have some…"

She opened the door. "Better go. Your *ewe* needs *you.*"

He walked away laughing, and once he'd driven away, Beth pulled the hen from the freezer. It would take an hour extra, perhaps more, for the bird to thaw and bake. So she set the oven gauge to 375° and the timer for 90 minutes. After centering the chicken in the blue-speckled roaster, she added half a cup of water and put on the lid.

While waiting for the oven to heat, she opened a jar of chicken stock, then began assembling the rest of the stuffing ingredients.

Earlier, she'd used another of her mother's recipes and prepared stuffed squash. The baking pan held nearly two dozen of the boat-like halves, more than enough to feed her family and Ben's. Once she'd cleaned up their dinner, Beth would pack up the squash, pies, and two-thirds of the fudge she'd made, and bring it to Hannah's. What a convenience, she thought, that her father preferred to eat early, and Ben's family ate late.

By the time Thomas returned from the barn, she had set his table.

"The lamb came easier than expected," he said, uncuffing bloodied shirt sleeves. When he noticed that she'd used her mother's best dishes, he nodded approvingly. "Aw, Emma would like this." Standing at the sink, he said over one shoulder, "And so do I."

High praise, coming from him. It took some of the sting out of missing her mother.

"Give me that shirt. Might take a few days to get it back to you, because blood stains can be stubborn."

He pulled it over his head, rolled it into a ball. "I am capable of soaking and scrubbing it."

"I know, but I want to do it."

"And I appreciate it." He dropped the ball into a plastic grocery bag and hung it on the back doorknob. "Now you cannot forget it."

Mirroring his playful smile, she said, "Did Mark get as messy as you did?"

"Worse, I am afraid. He insisted on doing most of the hard work alone. I suppose he sees the writing on the wall and wants to practice while I am here to teach and supervise."

"Writing on the wall? What does that mean!"

"We all know that someday caring for the flock will be Mark's responsibility."

The comment made her uncomfortable. "Then aren't we fortunate that you'll be around a long, long time teaching and supervising."

"To quote a tired adage, 'From your lips to God's ears.'"

He seemed so different today. Softer. Gentler. More loving and caring.

"Feeling okay, *Daed*?"

"Oh, a little tired, but that is normal after such a hard day."

"Is the lamb all right?"

"Oh, yes. Hale and hearty. He will grow into a healthy ram." He sniffed the air. "Everything smells good. How long until dinner?"

Beth glanced at the clock. "Fifteen, twenty minutes. I only need to whip the mashed potatoes and make some gravy."

"Then I have time to wash up and change into clean clothes?"

"And you won't need to rush."

Overhead, she heard his footsteps, doors and drawers opening and closing, and water rumbling through the old pipes. *What a relief that Mark decided not to move away*, she thought. Sharing the house was good for both of them, and her brother could keep a close eye on *Daed*.

Mark entered, as if on cue. Thomas hadn't exaggerated. His shirt, trousers, even his boots were covered in blood.

"Good grief," she said. "Did you perform a cesarean?"

"This looks worse than it is."

"But the ewe survived, right?"

"She's fine."

"Put your clothes in that plastic bag with *Daed*'s shirt. I'll take everything home and wash it."

"I hoped you'd say that," he said, returning from the mudroom.

Mark returned wearing pale blue longjohns. "Where's *Daed*?"

"Upstairs, washing up and changing clothes. That's what you should do, and while you're up there, remind him dinner is almost ready."

"Good. I'm famished."

"Before you go up, tell me… does *Daed* seem a bit under the weather to you?"

"No. Why?"

"He's just quieter and not at all grumpy."

"Don't be such a worrywart, Beth. He's not a youngster any more, and you know as well as I do how much effort it takes to birth a breech lamb."

"Wait. He told me you did the lion's share of the work."

"He was being generous. We shared the work. As for his good mood?" Mark rubbed his thumb and fingertips together. "The lamb is male, as good as money in the bank. I'm sure *Daed* is already thinking about how he'll spend the money it brings in."

With that, he turned the corner and made his way upstairs. Beth turned, too, to slide the biscuits into the oven. While pouring lemonade into tall tumblers, she hoped Mark had been right, and she'd only imagined the change in her father.

Perhaps Mark had also been right about the reasons for Thomas's uncharacteristic behavior. But in case he wasn't, it wouldn't kill her to stop by every few days just to make sure.

A bath and change of clothes improved her father's appearance. His energy, too. He ate with gusto and even had a second slice of pie for dessert.

"Everything was delicious, Beth." He shrugged into his coat. "I will be in the barn, checking on the ewe and her newborn."

"If I'm not here when you get back, I'll be at the Luttwylers' house, delivering the side dish and dessert I promised. Their dinner hasn't even started yet."

He pulled on his hat. "Give them my apologies."

"When I explain why you canceled, I'm sure they'll understand."

"And tell Amos he owes me a rematch at checkers."

"I'll do that. And tomorrow, I'll stop by to meet that baby."

Once he'd closed the door behind him, Beth faced her brother, who'd just helped himself to another piece of pie. "Will you do me a favor?"

He speared an apple slice. "Depends…"

She wondered if he knew how boyish he looked, grinning that way. "Check on *Daed* now and then, okay?"

"Sure. I have to make sure the chickens are in for the night anyway."

"Not just tonight, but tomorrow. And the next day. And the day after that."

"Worrywart," he said again. But Beth knew her brother well. He'd check on their father, probably so often that *Daed* would kick up a fuss.

By the time she made it to the Luttwylers', the entire family had already arrived. Beth delivered Thomas's apologies, along with the special message to Amos, who said, "Tell him I look forward to beating him again. I hope he never learns to say 'uncle.'"

"I hope you didn't eat too much at Thomas's," Hannah said, relieving Beth of the baking pan. "We have enough food here to feed the entire community."

"Oh, I hadn't planned to stay for dinner. I just wanted to bring—"

"What!" Ben interrupted. "You have to stay. I'd… *we'd* be disappointed if you didn't."

From the corner of her eye, Beth saw Hannah roll her eyes. And when the woman hid a giggle behind one hand, she got the distinct impression that, like Martha, Ben's mother believed romance was in the air.

And the fun didn't stop there. If they'd assembled a Ferris wheel and merry-go-round in the dining room, dinner would have been as festive as the county fair. Children's snickers harmonized with adult laughter, and good-natured jokes moved up and down the table as steadily as the overflowing bowls and platters of food.

Ben seemed so relaxed and calm. He teased his twin sisters and roughhoused with their kids, and they returned every joke with equal zeal. It was good to see him this way. And oh, how she'd enjoy being part of this affectionate bunch!

Her mother would have agreed.

Beth could almost see *Mamm*, walking behind each family member gathered at this table, reaching over their shoulders to drop heaping spoons of succotash and green beans onto each plate. And in her loving way, she'd stop now and then, use the corner of her apron to blot a gravy drip or cranberry smudge from the children's mouths. The image raised an ache in Beth's heart, and it threatened to well up and spill from her eyes.

What would her father say if he witnessed this? *"Stop living in the past. Your mother's death was God's will. Accept it once and for all."*

The imaginary lecture did nothing to stanch the stinging tears. "Be right back," she said, and hurried out to the front porch.

The wind caught fat snowflakes and whipped them into tiny twisters. Her mother would have loved this, too, she thought, hugging herself.

The door opened, and Ben said, "Beth? You okay?"

"I'm fine. And I'm sorry. Your family is just so wonderful. All that wonderfulness reminded me of how things were before I lost my mother and made me miss her a little more than usual. But I didn't want to spoil the fun, so I came out here."

~

"No need to apologize. And you're right. My family is wonderful. Crazy, but wonderful."

He noticed that she was shivering. And no wonder. The thermometer attached to the porch post read ten degrees. In her hurry to hide her tears, she'd forgotten her jacket.

Ben slipped out of his sweater and draped it across her shoulders.

"Oh, it's so warm and soft," she said, gathering it tightly around herself. "But what about you? You'll catch a chill for sure."

"I have more meat on my bones than you do, so it will take a good long while before I catch a chill."

"Well, thank you. I'm sorry for blubbering like a baby."

"One," he said, holding up a forefinger, "you are not blubbering." The index finger joined it. He aimed a thumb over one shoulder. "Two, they are in there, eating pie. With ice cream. I doubt anyone even noticed."

She laughed a little, and that pleased him. Ben searched his mind for something else to say, something that would encourage more of it.

"You are still shivering. How about going back in with me? You can warm yourself near the woodstove."

"I'm sorry," she said again. "You must be freezing out here in that thin cotton shirt."

Beth started to remove the sweater, but he placed both hands on her shoulders and stopped her. "We will go in when you are ready."

She exhaled a ragged sigh. "My mother has been gone nearly five years. You'd think by now I would've adjusted to life without her. As my father so often reminds me, her passing was God's will, and I'm showing a lack of faith, and weakness, wishing she was with us still."

"You are many things, Beth, but weak is *not* one of them." Hands still resting on her shoulders, he used his chin as a pointer. "Everyone around that table would feel exactly as you do if we lost my mother." Beth nodded. "You're such an understanding friend."

And there it was. The dreaded *friend* word. Should he tell her, right now, he wanted more than friendship? A *lot* more?

He pulled her close, so close he could feel her heart beating against his chest. It felt good, felt *right,* to hold her this way.

Ben cupped her chin in a palm and used his thumb to wipe away the tears that had clumped her thick lashes. "Beth," he whispered.

"Dear, sweet Beth…"

He leaned in to kiss her, but footsteps and the twins' voices stopped him. As the doorknob turned, her eyes widened and her mouth formed a perfect O. And when the interior door's hinges squealed, she whipped off the sweater and tossed it in his direction. It landed on his head, and as he struggled to uncover his face, the boys exploded onto the porch.

The first one said, "*Grossmammi* wants to know what you're doing out here."

His brother added, "And *Daed* said, 'Are those dunderheads trying to freeze to death?'"

Neither Ben nor Beth could answer, because his attempts to escape the sweater had left them both doubled over with laughter.

"They're not dunderheads," the first twin said, shaking his head, leading his brother back inside, "they're crazy!"

The screen door banged shut as Ben thought, *The boy is right. I'm crazy...* about Beth!

He'd used a contraction again. If that wasn't a sign of God's approval, he didn't know what was.

CHAPTER 10

The men had carried second helpings of pie into the parlor, and Ben's twin sisters went home to get the children bathed and ready for bed.

"I'll wash, you dry," Beth told Ben's mother, and rolled up her sleeves.

"You'll do no such thing," Hannah said. "You're a guest."

She held up both hands. "You'll be doing me a favor," Beth said, wiggling her fingertips. "Washing dishes will help soak this tinted varnish from under my fingernails." She adjusted the drain stopper and squirted soap into the sink. "And since I don't know where anything goes, it makes sense for me to wash while you dry and put way."

Hannah opened a cupboard drawer, withdrew a blue-checked towel. "I suppose your way *is* more productive."

While they worked, Hannah entertained Beth with "Ben as a Boy" stories:

At six, he got stuck high in the branches of the giant oak out back. "He'd been up there nearly six hours before Amos called the fire department. The twins asked the firefighters how many boys they'd rescued from trees. 'We're used to cats,' said one who carried Ben down, 'but this is our first boy.' And to this day," Hannah continued, "if the girls want to get his goat, they call him Cat Boy."

Ben had just turned nine when he decided to test his pitching skills by aiming at a waist-high chip in the barn wall. "The ball hit a window and shattered it. So if you hear the twins call him Big Hitter, you'll know why."

The stories continued as Hannah dried and plates and placed them on open shelves above the sideboard.

"So tell me, Beth, what were you like as a girl?"

"Not nearly as interesting as your son. When I wasn't helping my mother with housework, or caring for my father's sheep dogs, my nose was buried in a book."

"What did you do for pleasure?"

"I loved playing jacks indoors or hopscotch if the teacher insisted that we make use of the schoolyard. I'm afraid I wasn't very out-doorsy."

"I'm glad to hear you made time for fun. Playtime is important. It's also how parents teach children 'Do your best, or it won't be allowed.'"

"My mother made learning so enjoyable. She taught me to sew, making clothes for the dolls she sold in her shop. She was so patient and kind that I had no idea I was working."

"Ah, I remember Emma's little store. In fact, I bought the twins' first dolls from her. But tell me, how did stitching doll clothes turn into a full-time upholstery business?"

"Once, while my mother was out shopping, I spilled coffee on the sofa. I wasn't supposed to drink the stuff. I tried vinegar. Dish soap. Laundry detergent. Nothing lifted that stubborn spot. So I hid it, using material my mother had ordered by mistake, an ugly brownish-beige that couldn't be used for dresses, shirts, or trousers. But perfect for covering those cushions."

"And when Emma saw the cover?"

Smiling at the memory, Beth said, "She praised my stitchwork. And seemed more upset that I'd used up the last of her coffee grounds than she was about the sofa."

"That doesn't surprise me. Emma was a lovely, kind-hearted woman."

"Yes..." Beth couldn't say more, at least not without getting teary-eyed. Again.

"It's only natural you miss her." Pausing, Hannah said, "Is that why you left the table so suddenly earlier? Something reminded you of her?" Beth nodded.

Hannah drew her into a sideways hug. "You remind me so much of her. Your hair and eyes, your sweet disposition. I hope that when it's my time to join Jesus, Rebecca and Sarah and Ben will miss me as much." Whispering, she added, "Do you think such a hope is sinful?"

"If it is, I'll be guilty of it, too... if I'm ever blessed with children."

"Oh, you will be. I'm certain of it." She wondered *why* Hannah was so sure.

"I'm talking out of turn, but my son has feelings for you. I've seen it in his eyes, heard it in his voice. Eventually, he'll admit it to himself. At least that's my hope." Hannah dried a pot and bent at the waist to slide it onto a low shelf. Straightening, she whispered, "And I hope it's soon, because nothing would please me more than adding a third daughter to the family."

"What is all this whispering about?"

"Benjamin!" Hannah said. "How does a man your size—wearing big heavy boots—enter a room quiet as a cat?"

"Sorry if I startled you." Standing on Beth's other side, he eased his pie plate and fork into the sudsy water. "I just wanted to let you know the snow is falling harder. It is already too deep for you to walk home, so I will drive you."

"Oh, that's a good idea, son." Hannah handed the towel to Beth. "Dry your hands and get into your coat. We're nearly finished, so it'll take me no time to do the rest."

Beth looked up at him. "But I'm wearing winter boots. Walking home won't be—"

"I will start the truck right now, so it will be warm by the time you have said your goodbyes."

Rather than waiting for a reply, he took his jacket and hat from the coat rack and went outside.

"See?" Hannah said. "He's worried about you."

"Because he's such a caring man."

His mother submerged the last pot into the sudsy water. "Yes, he is. But I'm still going to pray that *this* is the night he'll come to his senses and tell you how he feels." She winked and said, "Now go, before he starts calculating how much gasoline he's burning."

Beth gave her a heartfelt hug. "Thank you so much, Hannah, for making me feel like part of the family."

"I hope that, soon, you won't just feel *like* part of the family." Smiling, she gave Beth a gentle shove. "I'll return your plates on the first sunny day so I can see your freshly painted kitchen."

Outside, Ben had shoveled a path from the porch to the walk and the driveway. Now, he stood beside the open pickup door. When she reached him, he helped her climb up into the cab.

"So tell me," he said, shifting into Drive, "how many tall tales did my mother tell about me?"

"Every word was complimentary." And the tales only made Beth like him more.

"Hmpf," he said. "It is a sin to lie, you know."

She heard the teasing smile in his voice. "No, really. She thinks the world of you."

"Hmpf," he repeated. "Then what was all the whispering about?"

"She, ah, I had asked her to share a secret family recipe." And she had… as the dishwashing began.

"I hope you repaid the favor by telling her how to make your fudge." Yet again, she knew he was smiling.

As he steered into her driveway, the truck's tires crunched over the snow. His bootsteps crunched, too, while he jogged around the pickup to open the passenger door. Reaching up, he gripped her waist and lifted her from the seat as if she weighed no more than a bag of sugar. In the moment it took to place her on the ground, their lips nearly touched. Disappointment filled her heart when they didn't. If he'd kissed her, she would gladly have returned it. *At least have the decency to feel guilty about it!* she told herself.

"You go on ahead," he said, slamming the door. "Stoke the fire while I clear away some of this white mess."

"I'll clean it up tomorrow after the snow stops falling."

He reached into the truck bed for a shovel. "By morning, you will have twice as much to move. Now go inside and warm yourself by the fire." Resting the tool's handle on one shoulder, Ben used his free hand to turn her toward the house. "You can thank me with a slice of apple pie, if there is any left."

"There is."

"And coffee?"

"That, too."

"Good. Now let me get to work."

After hanging up her coat, Beth opened the woodstove door and used the poker to stir the coals. A few pumps of the bellows breathed life into the embers, then she reached into the kindling bucket and tossed in a few twigs and sticks. The glow intensified, and she added a log. *Only three left. Better take care not to smother the fire.*

She was at the sink, washing her hands, when movement on the other side of the window caught her eye. It was Ben, flinging snow like a human plow. Ten minutes later, the sound of logs clunked onto the floor of the covered porch. How like him to make sure she'd have easy access to more! A few seconds later, he entered the kitchen, covered in snow and carrying an armload of wood. *Show me what I did to deserve him, Lord, and I'll do it again and again.*

Beth hung his coat on the hook near the stove. "It'll dry while you eat pie," she said as he sat.

He picked up the fork. "You are a woman of many talents, but a poet? That is a new one."

"Poet? *Me*?"

"'Dry… pie'?"

She sat, pointed at the window over the sink, and pretended she hadn't heard his latest joke. "Look how fast it's coming down. At this rate, we'll have another six inches on the ground by the time you finish. Let me wrap it up so you can take it with you."

"I cannot decide which offends me most…" He popped a chunk of pie into his mouth. "That you are trying to get rid of me, or your insinuation that I am a poor driver."

The twinkle in his dark eyes told her that Ben had been teasing. Again.

"You got us here, so I have confidence in your driving skills."

"Meaning, you *are* trying to get rid of me."

"Only because I don't want you getting stuck in a snowdrift."

"I think there is more to it than that." He took a slow sip of his coffee and then laughed. "All the gossips are tucked safely in their homes, Beth. No one knows I am here."

"You won't think it's funny when one of them tells your mother that you were seen cavorting with an unmarried woman. Without a chaperone."

"Maybe we should get married, steal all the joy from their rumor-mongering."

Now really, she thought, *how am I supposed to react to* that?

"How old are you, Beth?"

"What? I… I'll be twenty-eight in February." She failed to see what age had to do with anything. "And *you*?"

"Seven years your senior."

Thirty-five, she calculated. "And?"

"And surely you were taught to respect your elders…"

Beth groaned. "Seven years hardly makes you an *elder*."

"My father is ten years older than my mother, and they get along great."

"Where *are* you going with this line of thought?"

He waved the fork over his pie. "Merely pointing out that at my age, I see things a bit differently than you. You and I…" Now, he used the fork as a pointer. "…we know that nothing untoward is going on between us. If the neighbors choose to pollute their minds with rumor and innuendo, let them seek God's forgiveness."

Ben scraped the last of the dessert from his plate. "That was delicious. You could sell your pies. They are that good."

"Is that your subtle way of asking for another slice?"

"Good grief, no thank you." Ben moaned, pushed the plate away, and patted his flat stomach. "I could not eat another bite."

"Then I'll wrap some up for you to take home."

"I would rather eat it here with you."

Was Hannah's hope—that Ben would "come to his senses"—becoming reality?

"What are your plans for the weekend?" he asked.

"I'll cook a few meals for my father's freezer. Balance my checkbook. Housework. Laundry."

"I do not have that problem." He glanced around her kitchen. "My entire apartment would fit into this room."

"Do you wish it was bigger?"

"Only when I am in it, feeling cramped and bumping into things. People think of me as a hard worker. What they do not know is, staying busy lets me avoid being there."

With his woodworking and carpentry skills, why hadn't he made it larger? Why, he had the talent to build a two-story house.

He leaned both elbows on the table. "Do you ever regret moving out of Thomas's house?"

"No. Living on my own means I can stay up sewing all night without worrying that the machine will keep him and Mark awake. Plus, here in my own home, I can hang as many Christmas decorations as I please."

He wrapped both hands around his mug. "Ah-ha. So Thomas and I see eye to eye about such things."

A statement, she noticed, not a question.

"My mother loved Christmas. If not for his unbending rules, she would have baked and decorated, made and wrapped gifts for friends and family, and decorated as much as our Amish rules allowed. I never knew anyone more cheerful. The only time I ever saw sadness on her face was at Christmastime… especially on Christmas Eve."

"Why then?"

"Because she knew that's when others were exchanging gifts with loved ones, while Mark and I were holed up in our rooms, like any ordinary night, reading or working puzzles, and she sat making customers' dresses and aprons, shirts, and trousers."

Ben shook his head. "I did not know her well, but your mother struck me as the type who saw complaining as futile."

"You're right. The only time she complained was when her scissors were dull or her bobbin ran out of thread."

"Then… why did she let you see that your father's rules made her unhappy?"

Ben was treading on dangerous ground here, speaking ill of her mother. "She didn't *let* me see," Beth defended. "If we hadn't been so close, I might not have noticed little changes in her, like the way her eyes dimmed a bit when we passed houses with candles glowing in the windows or the hitch in her voice when she returned friends' *Freulich Kristag!* holiday greetings."

"I take it she enjoyed the pageant as much as you?"

"More. Until this year, the children wore her costumes. Remember that horrible rain storm last spring?" Ben nodded.

"Well, the schoolhouse roof leaked and soaked the storage cartons. When Leah opened them this fall and discovered that everything had grown moldy, she said 'The stains and smell will never wash out!' So I offered to make new ones."

"Let me guess. You also offered to donate plastic bins to store them in after the program."

"It just so happens that I had extras stacked in my storeroom."

"And you contributed them as an example of your Christmas spirit?"

He wasn't smiling when he said it and that riled Beth more than what he'd said about her mother. *He'll never change his attitude about Christmas, not even for you.* And since she'd long ago decided not to spend her life under the thumb of an unreasonable, uncompromising man, this discussion was pointless.

"In your mother's shoes, how would you have changed things?"

She met his steady gaze with one of her own. "I would have told my husband that marriage is give-and-take, and remind him that promises made before God and the entire congregation included honor and respect, which means accepting one another's… quirks."

You don't owe him an explanation. She got to her feet, collected his plate and half-filled mug and carried them to the sink. "My mother never took kindness for granted. Knowing how my father felt about things, she would have been overjoyed if he'd allowed her to hang a length of garland on the porch rail, a wreath on the door, or place one candle in a window. After all the loving kindnesses she performed for him every day, why couldn't he have given her that gift?"

She'd blurted it all out so quickly that she didn't realize tears had filled her eyes… until Ben got up, crossed the room, and stood facing her.

"Beth, I am sorry. I did not mean to make you cry."

"Not as sorry as I am for letting you *see* me cry." Using the hem of her apron, she blotted her eyes. A self-conscious giggle slipped from her lips. "If only it was springtime. I could blame this on allergies."

He lifted her chin on a bent forefinger. "You are the strongest woman I know. A tear or two, shed in memory of your mother, is not a sign of weakness."

Oh really? was her silent question. *Then what* is *it a sign of?*

As if he'd read her mind, Ben said, "It is a sign of love, the purest, sweetest kind."

He'd said as much on his mother's porch earlier. Just now, he'd apologized for upsetting her. If the worried look on his handsome face was any gauge, he'd meant it then, and he meant it now. *What more do you want from the man*?

The answer was simple: She wanted—no, *needed*—proof that if their friendship became more, Ben would be the husband she'd described, the type who would respect her wishes, even if he disagreed with them.

The question now was… could Beth accept Ben's stance on Christmas?

The answer, she decided, would require careful thought and heartfelt prayer. And while she was at it, she'd pray for guidance on whether or not her feelings for Ben were within His will for her life … and his.

But what was she thinking? Except for his "Maybe we should get married" joke, Ben had never said anything to indicate he wanted a future with her. She already felt silly enough for letting herself believe he might have feelings for her.

"It's been a long day," she said, "and after shoveling and hauling wood for me, you must be exhausted."

"Beth…"

She walked toward the woodstove, felt the sleeves of his jacket. "Not completely dry…" She held it out to him.

"Beth, you should know that—"

"…but not so damp that you'll catch a chill driving home."

His brows drew together, and his lips formed a thin line as he took it. "All right, I will go."

Beth needed to prove to him that, in addition to her mother's enthusiasm for Christmas, she'd also inherited her grateful spirit. He was half in, half out the door when she said, "Thank you, Ben. For driving me home. For shoveling. For bringing in enough wood to last until long after the snow stops."

"No, thank *you,* for letting me do it." A long brittle moment passed before he added, "Do you know how much I enjoy doing things for you?"

Memories flicked through her mind: Ben insisting on lifting heavy things, even things that before their part-time partnership, she'd moved herself. Ben saying, "Let me get that for you," every time she'd stood on tiptoe to fetch something from a high shelf. Ben carrying bags of material scraps to the trash bin. Had he performed each kind gesture, not only because he was a good and decent man, but because—

"If you were not so competent and efficient," he said over the pickup's roof, "I would do even more."

And then he walked away, leaving nothing but the imprints of his boot soles in the new-fallen snow.

Beth walked to the edge of the top porch step, arms crossed to fend off the chill and started to apologize for behaving like a self-centered, ungrateful brat. But he'd already closed the door, and he wouldn't have heard her over the rumbling engine.

The peculiar green lights of the truck's dash lit his face as he frowned, looked over his shoulder, and backed out of the drive. She waved, just in case he might see it as he steered onto the road. She watched until his taillights became tiny red dots in the darkness. And when the steadily falling snow swallowed them up, she went back inside…

…and prayed that she hadn't just destroyed any hope that somehow, someday, they'd come to a mutually satisfying meeting of their Christmas minds.

CHAPTER 11

Work had been slow, so three weeks had passed since Ben had seen her. At least, up close and personal.

Once, while driving past her house, he saw her at the mailbox. He'd slowed, tooted the horn… just a small tap, so as not to startle her. Unfortunately, she jumped anyway. He'd felt foolish, holding his breath and mouthing "Sorry" as he waved, and his heart sank when she raised an arm and quickly turned away.

That half-hearted hello had haunted his dreams every night since.

He'd seen her at church, of course, but she hadn't looked his way.

Twice in the church basement, while putting the finishing touches on the wooden risers, he'd almost caught her eye. Almost. And though they'd worked just a few yards apart, Beth on the costumes, he on the manger scene, she'd avoided eye contact.

During one of those sleepless nights, Ben made a decision, and it hadn't come easy: If celebrating Christmas meant that much to her, he'd set aside his feelings about the holiday. Eventually, he'd get used to gifts and decorations, but he knew he'd never get used to life without her.

But how could he tell her all that if she wouldn't even *look* at him?

Mercifully, on the way home from his last visit to the church basement, an idea dawned: His mother had long admired a sagging, shabby wingback chair in his shop. He would've fixed it up and given it to her by now, but other jobs that paid the bills had taken precedence. He went straight to work on it, removing material and padding, repairing the rickety frame, replacing springs. If he could talk Beth into helping with the upholstery, he could give it to his mother for Christmas.

Would seeing his change of heart bring about a change in *Beth*'s heart?

First thing the next morning, Ben loaded the chair into the back of his truck and made a beeline for Beth's shop. He found her at the work table, hand stitching the final seam of a fringed throw pillow. Beside it, matching cushions she'd already finished. Pale blue. Yellow. Cream. Each with a tufted button in its center.

When she saw him struggling to fit the chair through the door, Beth left her work and crossed the room. “Another of your roadside finds?” she asked, holding the door open.

“Yes,” he said, placing it near the workbench, “but this one has been in my shop for months.”

“Is this the one that had big ugly cabbage roses all over it?”

He nodded.

“And arms that leaned this way and that?” She measured an inch with her thumb and forefinger. “And timeworn cushions that were this thin?”

“One and the same.”

So far, she was behaving like the Beth he’d known before Thanksgiving night, and he thanked God for that.

“My mother saw it, and said if I ever got around to fixing it up, she would put it next to the fireplace in the parlor. ‘The perfect place to read, or knit, or stitch torn shirtsleeves,’ she said. And since I have time, now that my part in preparing for the pageant is over, I thought… I hoped…” He was stammering and knew it, but couldn’t seem to stop himself. "…I wondered, if you have the time, will you teach me how to upholster it… so I can give it to her… as… as a… a Christmas gift?"

"Give a Christmas gift? *You?*"

Beth had every right to look surprised—and a bit cynical. But he didn't have to like it. "My mother deserves a comfortable place to sit and relax at the end of a long day. If I can give it to her…"

Beth closed the door, rubbed her palms together. "Are you busy now?"

"No, but I never expected you to drop everything and start right away."

"Christmas is only a week away, so hang up your coat, and we can get started." She motioned for him to follow her into the storeroom. There, Beth pointed at the wall of floor-to-ceiling shelves, where she'd organized material by weight, pattern, and color. "Your mother might like something like this," she said, patting a bolt. "When I was at her house on Thanksgiving, I noticed that she likes muted tones. This plaid is just Plain enough to pass muster, even with the bishop. And it won't clash with her braided rugs."

"You are the expert."

Ben started rolling up his shirt sleeves and followed her back to the shop, where Beth handed him a tape measure, a tablet, and pencil. She walked a slow circle around the chair, then gave it a good shake. "You've already secured the wood joints and replaced the springs. That'll save us a lot of time."

Us. She'd said *us.* At the moment, nothing could have pleased him more.

She pointed at the tablet. "Before I start cutting the fabric, I'll need precise numbers. Height, width—the back, inside and outside—as well as the wings and arms." She paused. "Do you think your mother would like button-tufting? Or brass nailhead trim on the wings and arms?"

"You are the expert," he repeated.

Ben hoped she'd see that if he was willing to cooperate on a Christmas gift, of all things, he could alter his stance on Christmas. So he got busy calculating the chair's dimensions. While he worked, Ben tried to recall the upholstery terms she'd recited while they'd repaired sofas, settees, and dining chair seats. "Fabric backing…" he said under his breath, "is the white sheet that goes between the padding and the fabric." He winced. "No, not padding. *Weft*."

Beth returned and deposited the fabric and a bag of welting on the work table. She glanced around the shop. "Did a customer come in while I was back there?"

"Ah, no…"

"Hmm. I would've sworn I heard you talking to someone."

"Only myself." He held up the tablet that now held his measurements.

She took it from him, scanned his rough sketch of the chair and the sizes he'd penciled along each side.

"How late can you stay?" she asked.

"You think we can finish today?"

"We can, and we will."

"Then I will stay as long as it takes."

It had been just past ten when he'd shoved the dilapidated chair into her shop. They'd wasted no time, layering the batting and securing it into place. She hadn't complained as Ben struggled with every stitch and seam. Instead, Beth worked a little faster. "I'll do the sewing," she'd said. "You can hammer the brass nails into place."

The sun was setting when she said, "Well, that does it." They stood side by side, admiring their work.

"It looks as good as anything on the Gregan-Crawford showroom floor," he said.

"That's high praise. Their furniture is quality stuff!" Beth sat in the chair, hands resting on its arms. "It's quite comfortable, if I do say so myself." She paused, then added, "Do you think she'll like it?"

"I am certain of it."

On her feet again, she stood beside him. "What if it's too big for her parlor?"

"It will fit perfectly. And if it does not, knowing my mother, she will make it fit."

Ben slid a fingertip from her shoulder to her wrist, then clasped her hand. "Thank you, Beth. When she sees this, my mother will—"

The door opened with a bang, and her brother rushed inside. "Beth," he said, breathless and red-faced, "you have to come with me, right now."

She went to him. "Mark? What's wrong?"

"It's *Daed.* He fell. He'd gone upstairs to get into dry boots—we'd been shoveling all afternoon—and I heard a thump. Found him on the floor, unconscious. I dialed 9-1-1. The paramedics are with him now. Said things don't look good." He met Ben's eyes. "Only one of us can ride with him in the ambulance, so will you drive Beth to the hospital?"

"Of course. Yes. Definitely."

"Thanks," he said. And on his way out the door, Mark faced Beth, "See you there."

Ben didn't like the way she looked… pale, shaking, blinking… He guided her back to the chair, told her to sit, then raced around, adjusting the woodstove's damper, turning out lights, helping her into her coat. Mark had said things didn't look good for Thomas. It didn't seem right, offering false hope, so Ben locked the door and led her to his pickup.

Without a word, Beth pulled herself up into the cab. He couldn't think of anything to comfort her, so Ben started the engine and began reciting the Lord's Prayer. Beth joined in when he reached "…and forgive us our trespasses as we forgive those who trespass against us…"

She fell silent so suddenly that he leaned forward to make sure she hadn't fainted.

"After all this time, after all these years," she whispered, "he wasn't angry all the time. We were just beginning to build a new relationship, and now…"

Ben couldn't remember being so lost for words. He reached over the console and gave her hand a loving squeeze. And Beth squeezed back.

He parked in a space near the hospital entrance, and as they walked across the parking lot, hand in hand, Beth couldn't seem to take her eyes off the ambulance out front.

"Do you think it's the same one that brought *Daed* here?"

"Maybe."

As they approached, the automatic doors hissed opened, and she froze in her tracks.

"Oh no," she whimpered, her free hand atop her head. "I ran out of the shop so quickly, I forgot my *kapp*."

"It doesn't matter. No one will care."

"'Doesn't' instead of 'does not'?"

A faint smile lifted the corners of her mouth. "You're right. Contractions do save time. Now let's get you inside, okay?"

Right away, they saw Mark, sitting in a row of blue-plastic chairs, elbows on his knees, head in his hands. Ben sat on one side of him, Beth on the other. She slid an arm across his shoulders. "Have you heard anything more?"

Without looking up, he shook his head. "The doctor made me come out here. Said I'd only be in the way while they ran tests."

"In the way?" Beth said. She got to her feet, flung her coat onto the chair. "I'm going back there and get some answers, right now."

She looked over her brother's head, caught Ben's eye. "Stay with him?" she mouthed.

And Ben mouthed back, "I will."

He went to her, wrapped her in his arms, and kissed her forehead. "Go, get in their way. Mark and I will be here praying."

Chin up and shoulders squared, Beth walked purposefully through the double doors.

Mark watched as the doors closed behind her. "I wish God had blessed me with strength like hers. I'm a mess."

Sitting beside him again, Ben said, "You are doing fine."

"When my mother died, Beth held us together. She made all the arrangements, took care of *Daed* and me, took care of *everything.* Even after she bought the cottage and moved away… she kept taking care of us."

The information came as no surprise to Ben. He wondered if Mark had even noticed how hard tonight's news had hit her?

The question made him consider his own parents. Amos had always been healthy and strong, and God willing, he'd stay that way for many years to come. The same was true for his mother.

Why did it take a tragedy like this to wake people up? Make them admit the truth in the "Life is Short" adage?

From now on, Ben decided, he'd prove how much he appreciated every moment with them. He'd visit more often, *just because,* and not because they expected him to join them on holidays and for Sunday dinner.

"What's taking so long?"

Mark's question interrupted Ben's reflections, and when the

younger man started pacing, he said, "A few years ago, my grandmother was hospitalized. We waited for hours while they drew blood, took x-rays and scans. Waited hours more for the results."

Nodding, Mark exhaled a shaky sigh. "And what were the results?"

Should have kept your mouth shut, Ben thought, because now he'd have to admit that his grandmother had passed away before anyone could tell them why. Hemorrhagic stroke, they'd called it.

"I'm going back there and see what's keeping Beth." He took a few steps and stopped to say, "You can leave if you want."

"No, I will stay. I want to hear the news, too." Hopefully, whatever had caused Thomas's fall wasn't serious, and soon, he'd bring all three of them home.

Now, alone in the waiting room, it was Ben who walked back and forth, from the entrance to the registration desk and back again, praying with every step that when Beth and her brother returned, they'd look happy and relieved.

His pacing must have annoyed the clerk, because she asked, "Is everything all right, sir?"

He wanted to bellow, "No, it is not!" Instead, he said, "Yes. Fine.

Thanks."

Ben sat down, picked up a dogeared magazine, and flicked through its pages without really seeing what was printed on them. He walked down the hall, found a coffee machine, and slid a bill into the slot. "Highway robbery," he muttered. "Could have bought half a pound of ground coffee with that dollar."

Ben returned to the same chair. Drained the paper cup. Leafed through the entire stack of periodicals by the time the double doors opened again. Mark and Beth, arm in arm, trudged toward him, dropped heavily into chairs on either side of him. Ben didn't need to ask about Thomas's condition. Their pained expressions said what words needn't: Thomas Lantz had died.

He extended a hand, and Beth put hers into it. "We have to come back tomorrow," she said, her voice a mere whisper, "with the mortician."

"Aw, Beth…" Ben knelt at her knees, wrapped both cold, trembling hands in his own. "I am sorry, so very sorry."

She leaned forward and rested her forehead against his chest. "I should never have moved away. Maybe… maybe if I'd been there, I would've noticed something. Insisted that he visit Dr. Baker."

"You heard the doctor," Mark said. "*Daed* died of ventricular fibrillation. No way you could have known he had an arrhythmia. Like the man said, *Daed* probably didn't pay any attention to it either."

Mark stood, picked up his coat, and picked up Beth's, too. Ben took it from him, helped her to her feet, and helped her into her coat, too.

"Let's get you home."

"Home," Mark echoed. "I… I can't. Okay if I stay at your house tonight, Beth?"

She sent him a sad smile, "Of course."

"Good idea," Ben said. "Neither of you should be alone tonight." *Or during the hard days ahead...*

As they made the short drive from Oakland to Pleasant Valley, no one spoke. No one cried either, and Ben thought he knew why: The Amish were expected to accept death as a routine part of life, like inhaling and exhaling. Loved ones lost were welcomed by the loving arms of Jesus, so sadness and tears were pointless. Their duty now, as believers, was to accept God's will and move forward.

Though he'd never admit it out loud, Ben thought it was outrageous and cruel to make people feel guilty for feeling grief, to deny them time to mourn the death of a spouse, a parent or sibling, even a beloved friend.

He parked in Beth's driveway, exactly where he had that morning. Mark exited the truck first, and trudged, slump-shouldered, to the porch and let himself in.

As Ben helped Beth climb down from the cab, she said, "Can you come in for a while? I'll make coffee. And there's pie."

"No need to feed me. I am happy just to be with you." He felt honored that she'd asked him to stay. And stay he would, for as long as she needed him.

Beth, Mark, and Ben sat at her kitchen table, sipping coffee, absent-mindedly poking at slices of apple pie, talking about the newborn lamb. The weather. The upcoming Christmas pageant. Everything and anything but how they'd spent the last six hours.

Upon the loss of his paternal grandparents, Ben had gone into town to help his father with final arrangements, and he'd done the same when his mother lost her parents. Mark told him that Beth had taken care of everything when their mother died. If he could spare her going through that heartbreaking task this time, he aimed to do it.

First thing tomorrow, he'd visit the bishop, who'd help organize Thomas's funeral. The man knew the Lantzes well enough to select favorite Bible verses and hymns, and tell the stone mason what to engrave on the grave marker.

He intended to stay with them after delivering the news that everything was taken care of.

And he'd stay with them every other step of the way, for as long as they needed him.

CHAPTER 12

The weeks following the funeral passed slowly. Beth didn't know how she and Mark would have coped without Ben's help.

Thanks to him, the only thing required of them was to be present as neighbors dressed Thomas according to his wishes in his Sunday clothes. Ben stood with them as friends filed by the dining room table, whispering condolences. And sat quietly in the church as the bishop assured congregants that their brother in Christ now resided with God in heaven. He'd been with them in the graveyard, one arm draped over Mark's shoulders, the other holding Beth close to his side.

Beth would never forget the way he pulled her closer as they lowered the Plain pine coffin into the ground and closer still as friends sang, "There's a City of Light."

All through the dinner that followed, he remained nearby, his strong presence proving what he'd said at the hospital: "I'll stay for as long as you need me."

Though she hadn't seen him since, Beth sensed that same presence, and knew that if she'd needed him, Ben would have come to her, to offer solace, a friendly ear, a shoulder to cry on. She smiled a little, thinking of the protective speech he'd delivered on the night of the funeral, when she apologized for breaking down. "Stop apologizing," he'd said. "You have every right to cry. It is shameful that *some* people make you feel guilty for grieving your father's passing."

Now, on this night before Christmas Eve, Beth sat at her desk, praying as her pen scratched across paper, asking God's guidance in choosing the right words. Words to thank him. Words to underscore his kindness and decency. Words that pointed out his talents and expressed regret for the pressure she'd put on him to celebrate Christmas *her* way. So many words, yet not one expressed how precious he was to her, how much she'd come to love him. No, far better to wait until she could look into his eyes to admit those things.

Setting the pen aside, Beth leaned back in the chair and stared at the gift she'd soon deliver… the special toolbox where Ben could store the treasured hand tools handed down from his grandfathers. She got up, found a roll of plain brown paper, and cut off enough to wrap it. Ordinary twine held the folds in place. At her desk again, she signed the letter, slipped it into an envelope, and tucked it under the rough-hewn bow. Tomorrow, after dark, she'd walk to his shop and quietly place it on the narrow porch that led to his tiny apartment.

What happened next, well, that was entirely up to the Good Lord.

~

Ben hadn't had a decent night's sleep in weeks. It seemed just as soon as he drifted off, thoughts of Beth would wake him. Was she crying into her pillow? Regretting missed opportunities to grow closer to her father?

He knew she'd miss the man, because that snowy day in the graveyard, as the last shovelful of dirt thumped onto his coffin, she'd leaned against his arm and said, "You know, I think I'll even miss his anti-Christmas sentiments."

No doubt she wondered what would become of her brother. Would Mark would live in the house he'd shared with Thomas? Would he take over the sheep farm? Would he sell the farm and the house to move in with her permanently?

The logs in the woodstove popped and crackled, a reminder that it was time to stoke the fire, add a few logs, and head to bed. It was nearly ten, and he wanted to take advantage of the drowsiness that had settled over him.

Yawning, Ben stepped outside to grab a few logs for the woodstove.

"Not a cloud in the sky," he said, looking into the inky, star-sprinkled vastness. He inhaled crisp mountain air, stacked short lengths of oak and locust in the crook of his arm. As he turned to go back inside, the toe of one boot thumped against something. Something that crinkled. Definitely *not* wood.

Curious, he reached around the doorframe and flicked on the porch light. The yellow bug light cast a golden glow across the snow and the weathered floorboards… and illuminated a brown-wrapped package. A day or so ago, his mother had asked when he planned to retire his scruffy old boots. How like her to surprise him this way with a new pair.

After dropping the wood beside the stove, he went to fetch the boot box. In the shadows of the porch light, he saw tiny footprints in the snow. Footprints exactly like those Beth's shoes had left on her sidewalk right before he erased them with his shovel.

Closing the door behind him, he carried the box into the kitchen. It wasn't until he placed the package on the table that he noticed the envelope. "To Ben," it said. He'd seen Beth's handwriting enough times to recognize it. He sat and took hold of the letter.

"Dearest Ben," it began, "I know how you feel about Christmas gifts, so let's call this an early birthday present." He wouldn't turn thirty-six until May. *A very early birthday present*, he thought, smiling as he read on. "If you see flaws in it, blame my lack of concentration. I tried to pay attention as you sawed and hammered and sanded, but maybe I paid a little more attention to your strong hands and handsome profile to commit the lessons to memory." He glanced at the box. So, she'd made this? Especially for him? With everything else she did, when had she found the time?

"You'll find a note inside the box, and it'll explain what it's for. Please, Ben, don't be angry with me for too long, because I simply had to do this for you!" And she'd signed it, "With much love, Beth."

Placing the letter aside, Ben tugged at the ends of the twine, and as the bow released, the brown paper fell away from the box. He picked it up, turned it over and around, inspecting the smooth, slightly glossy mahogany, the perfectly mitered corners, and brass hinges and clasp that had been expertly attached with minuscule brass nails. She'd woodburned his initials into the lid, too, and he traced them with a forefinger. Then, lifting the lid, he found the note she'd tucked inside. "To protect your treasured hand tools from loss and rust," it said.

She'd lined the interior with supple leather, and the seams, like everything else, met perfectly.

It was by far the most thoughtful, meaningful gift he'd ever received. Tears stung his eyes that she'd spent so much time and energy on it. How could she think it would make him angry?

But he knew the answer to that, and guilt hammered in his heart. He had to make things right.

But first, he needed to assemble the tools he'd set aside when Beth first expressed an interest in woodworking. The tools had been rusty and worn when he traded an antique mirror to get them. A little sanding, some varnish on the handles, and the set looked almost new again. He'd planned to deliver them on her birthday. *Plans change*, he thought, and slid the chisels, carving blades, and miter square into a rugged, brown-leather case. Ben snapped it shut, and using the brown paper that had covered his toolbox, wrapped and secured it with Beth's twine.

He gave a moment's thought to writing a letter. *No, better to speak what is in your heart in person.*

Ben put on his coat and hat, and because it was such a bright, clear night, decided to walk to her house. She was on the front porch when he got there, rocking in the big wicker chair, eyes closed, humming. He recognized the tune. Silent Night. He stood quietly, barely breathing, watching and listening. He'd been right: Her voice in song was beautiful. But then, he'd be hard-pressed to name something about her that wasn't.

Beth must have sensed his presence, for she opened her eyes, looked directly at him.

"You found your gift?"

"I did," he said, hiding the gift to her behind his back.

"If you aren't here to lecture me about the evils of gift-giving, I might consider inviting you in for coffee and pie."

She smiled as she said it, so Ben took the steps, two at a time. *Saves time, kind of like contractions.* Time was precious, he thought, and he'd allowed his stubborn pride to waste far too much of it. If things went as he'd prayed, that would change tonight.

"Did you find many mistakes?" she asked, pouring coffee into two mugs.

"It's perfect. *You're* perfect." He sat at the table, placing her present beside the mug. Before she had a chance to ask about it, Ben sandwiched her hands between his own. "I will treasure that toolbox, always. The time and effort that went into every inch of it, well, I'll treasure that, too. But you should know, it wasn't necessary, because…"

Standing, Ben brought her to her feet, cupped her chin in a palm and forced her to meet his eyes.

"…because *you* are the only gift I'll ever need, for the rest of my life."

Beth blinked, and as a tear slid down her cheek, she swiped it away. "I'm so glad you like it."

Ben pulled her close, rested his chin on her head. "Ah, Beth, Beth, Beth. I don't like it. I *love* it."

He sat again, pulled her into his lap, and handed her the package. "I know it isn't Christmas Eve when all you Christmas enthusiasts like to exchange presents, but I'd like you to open it."

She untied the twine. "You know, I've lost count of how many contractions you've used tonight."

"Every second I save using them is one more I can spend with you."

Beth was blushing when she removed the wrapper. Tossing it aside, she held the case in both hands, unsnapped it, and looked inside.

"A woodworking set?"

"A woodworking set," he echoed. "Seems fitting, since you've carved your name onto my heart."

Beth looked at the ceiling. "And he calls *me* a poet?"

He took the case from her, put it on the table, got to his feet again, and took her with him.

"I'm genuinely sorry for anything I said or did to make you think I could ever be angry with you. In fact, I can think of only one thing you could do to make me angry."

Both well-arched brows rose high on her forehead as she whispered, "What?"

"Say no."

"What?" she repeated, this time, because she didn't understand.

"I have enjoyed every moment of our time together, even the hard, blister-inducing moments. I admire and respect you. As God is my witness, *I love you.* Have, almost from the moment we put our heads and hands together on that first project, will for the rest of my days. If you'll have me, I want to spend every contraction-saving moment proving it."

He hugged her tighter. "Will you marry me, Beth?"

"May I store my chisels in the toolbox, alongside your hand tools?"

He grinned. "Yes, you may."

"And can I hang a wreath on our front door at Christmastime? Just one, and nothing more?"

"If it makes you smile like this," he said, pressing a fingertip to her lips, "you can drape the entire house in evergreen boughs."

She snuggled close. "I'd never do that to you." And looking up into his face, Beth said, "I think it's a sign from God that we share the same initials, don't you?"

He pictured the double L's she'd painted on the sign for their booth, that she'd woodburned into the lid of his toolbox.

"Yes, I think it is. Does that mean you'll marry me?"

Gently, she poked a fingertip into his chest, teased him with the list of things she could make with her new chisels. "I'm joking of course," she said. "I've been praying for this for months. I'm honored. Delighted. Grateful that God decided to answer my prayers, finally." Beth gave him another poke. "We aren't spring chickens, you know, so we probably shouldn't wait too long to start a family of our own. I only have one regret…"

"Say it isn't so…"

"I wish my mother and father could be here to see us marry, to welcome grandchildren. And Mark! He'll be so happy when we tell him. Why, I think—"

Ben silenced her nervous rambling with a long, slow kiss, and she melted into him.

ABOUT THE AUTHOR

Once upon a time, *USA Today* best-selling author Loree Lough sang for her supper, performing before packed audiences throughout the U.S. and Canada. Now and then, she blows the dust from her 6-string to croon a tune or two for the "grandorables," but mostly, she writes. (And writes.) Her stories have earned thousands of 5-star reviews, hundreds of industry and "Readers' Choice" awards, and 7 book-to-movie options. At last count, nearly 17,000,000 copies of Loree's books were in circulation, and by year-end of 2022, she'll have 146 books on the shelves. She and her husband split their time between a home in the Baltimore suburbs and a cabin in the Allegheny Mountains, where she continues to hone her "identify the critter tracks" skills.

http://www.loreelough.com

Progressive Rising Phoenix Press is an independent publisher. We offer wholesale pricing and multiple binding options with no minimum purchases for schools, libraries, book clubs, and retail vendors. We offer substantial discounts on bulk orders and discounts on individual sales through our online store. Please visit our website at:

www.ProgressiveRisingPhoenix.com

If you enjoyed reading this book, please review it on Amazon,
B & N, or Goodreads.
Thank you in advance!

CPSIA information can be obtained
at www.ICGtesting.com
Printed in the USA
LVHW051150170623
750060LV00012B/585

9 781958 640272